Remember, what matters the very most is not how big and tough you are, but the size of your heart!

Denise Coughlin

Bill Kartan

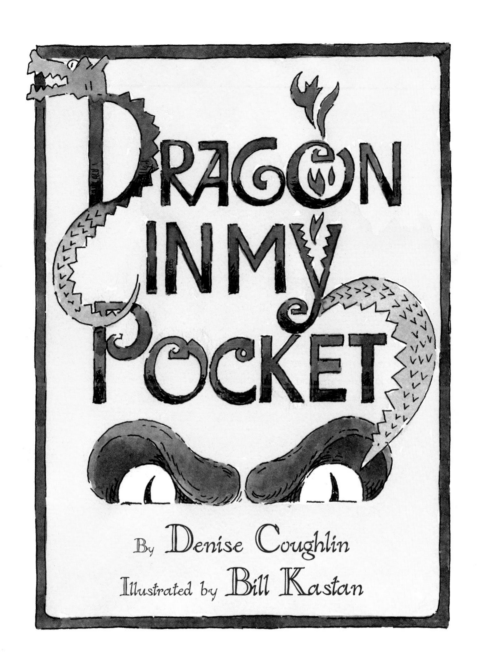

Dragon In My Pocket

By Denise Coughlin

Illustrated by Bill Kastan

Rose Valley Publishing

Sebastian imagined there was a dragon hiding in his closet. It was very large, with huge green scales, yellow eyes and extremely bad breath. He was afraid it was going to pounce on him the moment his mother turned out the lights in his room.

"I don't want to sleep, mom!" Sebastian exclaimed, eyeing the closet door. He read the clock beside his bed. It was nine o'clock.

"You need your rest, Sebastian," his mother said as she began to straighten his blankets. "I will read you another story if it will help you to stop worrying about dragons. You must stop thinking about them so much!"

Sebastian gave his mother a sad little smile then glanced at the closet door again. Next to the closet was the chess set his dad had given him. It was sitting on a table near his bed so he could see it. On the chessboard stood two miniature armies of knights.

Sebastian missed his dad very much. He was a captain in the air force and was away from home for several months at a time. His dad had brought the chess set from a city called Krakow when he visited Sebastian's grandmother's family. They had sent many gifts for Sebastian, including the beautiful chess set with the little armies of knights that made Sebastian think of a battle against an evil sorcerer.

"Does the nutcracker live in Krakow?" Sebastian had once asked Busia, his grandmother. That day in New York when his father had been on leave at Christmas, he had seen the Nutcracker Ballet with his family. On the way home from the show he had heard his dad talking to his grandmother about the country of Poland, where she had lived as a girl.

"No," his Busia had answered, "but there had once been a very brave young man named Krakus who lived in Krakow. I suppose you'd be interested to know he battled a very wicked dragon, my dear Sebastian. The courageous knights could not slay the evil dragon, but this very brave young man did by being very clever. He married the beautiful princess and became the king. I am told that is how the city of Krakow got its name."

Busia had made him giggle when she said the name of the city in Poland in her funny accent. Sebastian remembered seeing the lines in Busia's face that day and thinking she was very old. He wondered if perhaps Busia had really seen a fire-breathing dragon, because he had seen tears come to her eyes several times while she was peeling onions and looking out the window at his mother's garden.

Sebastian took a deep breath and looked at the closet again. He was worried about many things. Besides fire-breathing dragons and a few gruesome monsters he imagined sometimes hiding under his bed, he was worried about going to school. He didn't want to go because he was the smallest boy in his class and another boy named Nathan Monroe liked to tease him about being a baby. His mom explained that he was a late bloomer. At first Sebastian thought she was talking about one of the flowers in her garden. If she thought of him as a plant, Sebastian decided, he would prefer to be a prickly pear cactus rather than one of her rose bushes. Mom was always fussing over her roses. He was sure that a prickly pear cactus could get along just fine without people making a fuss over it. And he was sure it would scratch when people rubbed it the wrong way, especially a person like Nathan, who seemed to be mean all the time.

Last Tuesday when Sebastian had been standing in the lunch line next to the janitor's closet at school, the furnace let off a long burst of steam. Sebastian jumped and let out a squeal of surprise. At that very moment, he imagined a very LARGE fire-breathing dragon waiting to be fed hiding behind the steel door. And wouldn't you know it — mean old Nathan Monroe had been standing behind him. Sebastian hadn't meant to jump, but the hissing steam had been very loud. He took another step forward when the line moved only to trip over his untied shoelace. All he could remember now was his nose hitting the slippery old linoleum floor, staring at a piece of nasty-dried-up bubble gum ... and Nathan's singsong voice.

"Didn't mommy tie your shoes, baby?" Sebastian heard Nathan yell out behind him.

As the days went by and Nathan teased him more and more, then started to push him in the hall at school, Sebastian began to feel terribly sad. He sat at the kitchen table with Busia and looked out the window like she usually did. Many nights he could not finish his dinner because he kept hearing Nathan's voice in his mind calling him a "baby."

One day, Sebastian's mother rumpled his hair as she went by and handed a cup of tea to Busia. She said he and Busia looked like two of a kind staring out the window at the garden. She asked them what they were looking at.

"A tiny chipmunk sitting on the garden angel's head," Busia said. "He is such a sweet and gentle creature. Because the weather has gotten colder, he likes to sit on top of the angel in the sunshine and feel the warmth on his silky fur."

Sebastian didn't say anything to his mother. He felt quiet and prickly. He watched the tiny chipmunk jump down onto the garden angel's shoulder as his mother straightened the collar on his shirt. Suddenly Sebastian wished his mother would go away.

"Sebastian, I have wonderful news for you," his mother said. "Mrs. Wallace wants you to try out for the Christmas play this year. Don't you think that would be fun?"

Fun? Sebastian thought, feeling very sorry for himself. Why, he was so clumsy he would probably trip over his untied shoes and have everyone laugh at him. And he was sure he'd forget his lines like a baby would!

Busia patted his cheek gently with her hand. He could smell her perfume. He looked at her sadly, then out the window at the chipmunk. It was still sitting on the garden angel's shoulder.

"What are you thinking about, my dear Sebastian?" Busia asked. "You will have lines in your face like mine if you keep frowning like that. Why, you will even scare the chipmunk!"

"Dragons." Sebastian said, making a horrible face at the chipmunk, which was so unlike him.

"Dragons? Well my goodness," Busia said, taking a sip of her tea. "Is there a particular dragon that is troubling you?"

"All dragons." Sebastian said. "It feels like they are everywhere!"

Busia's eyes were full of understanding. "Yes, as I recall there are many different kinds of dragons," she said. "Of course there are good ones and bad ones. I suppose some of the very evil ones, and the ones that are not housebroken," Busia added hiding a smile, "can be quite troubling if you don't know how to handle them."

Busia walked into her bedroom and came back with a very small dragon made out of stone. She handed it to Sebastian.

"He's a very tiny dragon, Busia," Sebastian said in delight. He held the tiny dragon in the palm of his hand. It was just as big as one of his knights. "Where did you get him?"

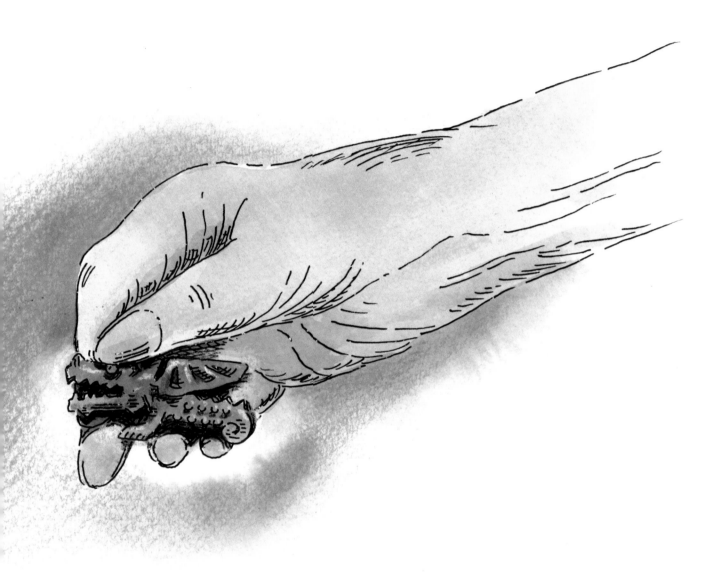

"I've had him for many years," Busia said. "I got him as a souvenir in Krakow when I was a young girl. I brought him to America in my pocket. I almost lost him once. I want you to have him now, Sebastian, to remind you who you are. Yes, when I was a girl, it was a very sad time. It felt as though a wicked dragon had taken over the land."

"What happened, Busia?" Sebastian asked.

Busia closed her eyes. She was very still. Finally she put her wrinkled hand over Sebastian's hand. "Always remember this, my sweet Sebastian," she said, opening her eyes. "Goodness and love are treasures like no others. They feed people's spirits. They make people grow strong and beautiful inside.

"Long, long ago when I was a young girl, it was as though a very wicked dragon had come to live in my country once again. This dragon thought that by stealing the people's spirits it would become bigger and more beautiful and never die. It thought that by making people afraid it would have power over them. But many people understood the most important thing they each had was their good

heart. They understood the most important things were not their homes or their toys, but their kindness and love.

"There were many good people who were very brave. They did not let this dragon steal their spirits because they were frightened. They protected their hearts," Busia said, putting her hand over Sebastian's heart. "They knew something very special, dear Sebastian. They knew what matters the very most is not how big and tough you are, but the size of your heart. The dragons that appear to frighten us will only get smaller and smaller when we let our brave and loving hearts get larger and larger."

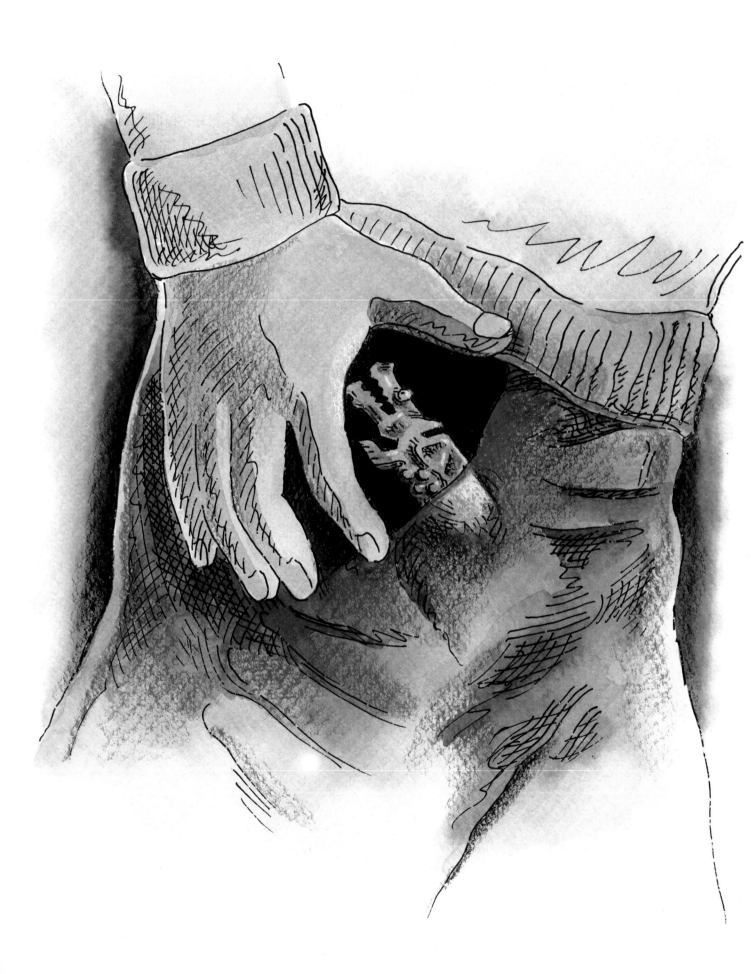

Busia took the little dragon from Sebastian and held it up in her wrinkled hand. "Only our brave and loving hearts can protect us when a dragon wants to make us afraid or hurt our spirit."

Sebastian slipped the tiny dragon Busia gave back to him in his pocket. He thought of a knight who wore bright and shiny armor to protect his noble heart. Suddenly he laughed at a funny thought he had when he looked at his father's telescope standing by the dining room window.

"Can you have a heart the size of the universe?" Sebastian asked, after glancing out the window at the sky. His dad had told him about the universe one day while they were looking through the telescope together.

Busia's blue eyes were twinkling brightly like the stars Sebastian had seen in his father's telescope. "When you let your heart grow as big as the universe," she said, rumpling his hair with her fingers, "then you will have a heart like God's heart, and you will gain understanding, Sebastian. You will be able to shrink any evil dragon in the world down to size."

The next day Sebastian told his mother he would like to try out for the Christmas play. A knight would be brave, he thought.

Sebastian's mother was very pleased. Two weeks later she and Busia drove him to the building where auditions for the play were being held. Inside there were many children of all sizes hoping to get a part. Sebastian was surprised to discover the play was called the Nutcracker Review.

PARTS NEEDED FOR NUTCRACKER REVIEW

Sebastian waited in line for quite a very long time. When it was his turn Mrs. Wallace made him stand as straight and tall as he could. She made him march across the stage.

"That's wonderful, Sebastian," she finally said. "You've really grown this year. I think you will make a fine toy soldier."

Proudly Sebastian glanced at the other children. He was surprised to see Nathan Monroe. He realized Nathan was trying out for the play too! Sebastian imagined he saw a dragon standing in line next to Nathan. He felt a shiver go up and down his spine.

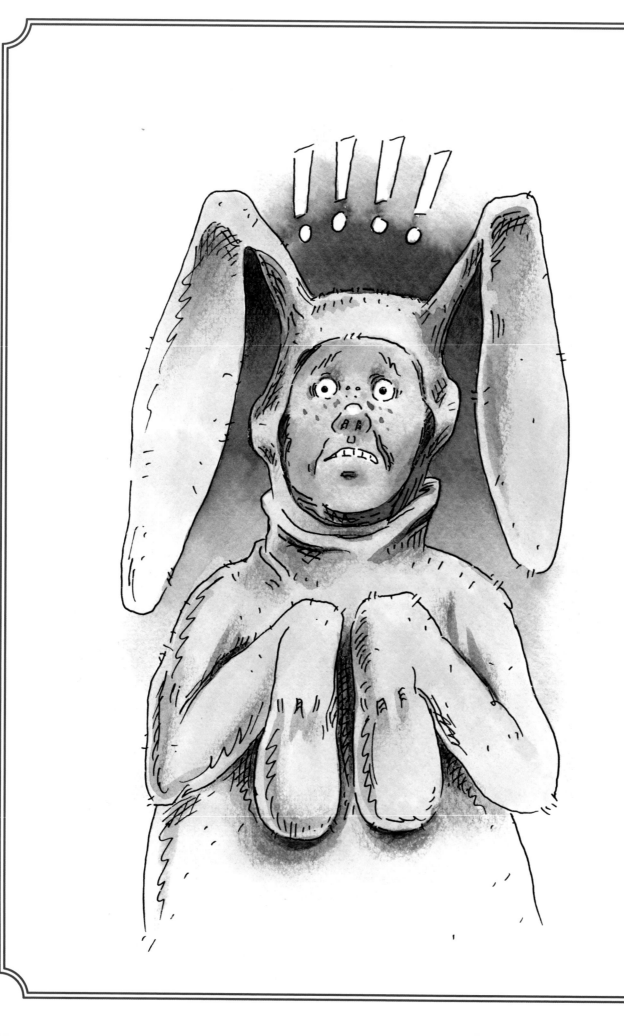

Mrs. Wallace called Nathan's name just then. She made him march across the stage like a toy soldier. After a minute or two, she smiled and told him to hop from one end of the stage to the other.

Finally Mrs. Wallace announced, "Nathan, I've saved a very special part for you. I think you will make a marvelous rabbit."

Sebastian couldn't believe his ears. Finally he burst into a huge grin. He realized Nathan Monroe was going to be the toy rabbit in the play. Sebastian imagined what mean old Nathan would look like in a rabbit costume. Suddenly he didn't seem so frightening anymore. In fact, Sebastian even felt a little sorry for Nathan, and wondered what had happened to make him so mean.

Sebastian closed his eyes and put his hand in his pocket. He touched Busia's little dragon for courage. In his mind, he saw his father smiling at him. When he opened his eyes, he looked at Nathan again and all the children standing around him. He thought of God's enormous loving heart. Then he thought of his own heart growing stronger and braver each day.

Suddenly he imagined all the dragons that had troubled him standing in a row on the stage. Grinning from ear to ear, Sebastian pictured them wearing bunny costumes like Nathan would in the play. Then he pictured all the dragons hopping across the stage like silly old rabbits in front of Mrs. Wallace. Sebastian couldn't stop smiling. He knew he would never be afraid of another dragon or monster or sad old bully like Nathan again. He understood what Busia had told him. With God's help and a brave and understanding heart he'd be able to shrink any dragon in the world down to size. Once again he touched the tiny dragon in his pocket and looked at Busia. He thought she was the greatest grandmother he had ever seen.

The End

This book was inspired by the life of Pope John Paul II, and my parents, Richard and Theresa Jachimowicz ... who taught me how to grow my heart.

Special Acknowledgements:

To my daughter Jessica who helped to make this book possible with all of her hard work.

To Mark Wells and Tom Krozak for their support of Szamatuly Orphanage and this book. They have truly helped to make a "Miracle" happen.

To my friend Carol Turgeon and her husband, Gerry, for their advice and technical support. Thanks once again.

Most of all to my husband Ken, who has supported my dream throughout our marriage.

Text copyright © 2005 by Denise Coughlin

Illustrations copyright © 2005 by Bill Kastan

http://www.rosevalleypublishing.com

Library of Congress Cataloging-in-Publication Data

Coughlin, Denise.
Dragon In My Pocket/by Denise Coughlin; illustrated by Bill Kastan. — Shelby Township, MI: Rose Valley Publishing, 2005.
p.; cm.
Audience: children ages 4-8.
Summary: A wise grandmother helps her small grandson find the courage he needs to face a bully and protect his own "good" spirit.
1. Courage—Juvenile fiction. 2. Bullying—Juvenile fiction. 3. Dragons—Legends—Juvenile fiction.
4. Folk literature, Polish—Juvenile fiction. 5. Legends—Poland—Juvenile fiction. 6. [Bullies].
I. Kastan, Bill. II. Title.
PZ7.C684 D73 2005
[E]—dc22 0506

ISBN 0-9765905-0-6
Printed in Canada by Friesens
First printing, May 2005
Layout/Design by Jessica Kerr